All children have a great ambition to read to themselves... *and a sense of achievement when they can do so.*

The **read it yourself** *series has been devised to satisfy their ambition. Since many children learn from the Ladybird Key Words Reading Scheme, these stories have been based to a large extent on the Key Words List, and the tales chosen are those with which children are likely to be familiar.*

The series can of course be used as supplementary reading for any reading scheme.

The Ugly Duckling *is intended for children reading up to Book 3c of the Ladybird Reading Scheme. The following words are additional to the vocabulary used at that level –*

summer, by, duck, her, nest, she, eggs, little, crack, out, ducklings, egg, big, cracks, duckling, not, ugly, all, swim, farm, ducks, but, do, sad, away, runs, marsh, there, sees, looks, am, cold, house, cannot, swan, winter, ice, children, live, goes, spring, fly, grown

British Library Cataloguing in Publication Data

Ainsworth, Alison
The ugly duckling.—(Read it yourself. Level 3; v. 8)
1. Readers—1950-
I. Title II. Holmes, Stephen III. Series
428.6 PE1119

ISBN 0-7214-0867-2 (Hardback)
ISBN 0-7214-8265-1 (Paperback)

Published by Ladybird Books Ltd Loughborough Leicestershire UK
Ladybird Books Inc Auburn Maine 04210 USA

Printed in England

The Ugly Duckling

retold by Alison Ainsworth
illustrated by Stephen Holmes

Ladybird Books

It is summer.

The birds and rabbits play by the water.

Here is a duck on her nest.

She has some eggs in the nest.

One by one,
the little eggs crack.
Out come some little ducklings.

The duck says,
Come to me, little ducklings.

One egg is big.
This egg cracks.
Out comes a big duckling.

The duck says, You are not
like the little ducklings.
You are a big ugly duckling!

The duck and all the ducklings go to the water.

They all swim up and down.

They have fun in the water.

The duck says to the ducklings,
We have to go to the farm.
The big ducks want to see you.

On the farm the big ducks say,
We like the little ducklings,
but we do not like the big
ugly duckling.

The ugly duckling is sad.

The little ducklings
have fun on the farm.
The ugly duckling
wants to play.

But the little ducklings say,
You are a big ugly duckling.
We do not want to play with
you.
Go away!

The ugly duckling is sad.

He runs to the marsh.

There he sees some
big marsh ducks.

One big marsh duck comes
to look at the ugly duckling.

You do not look like me,
says the big marsh duck.
Look into the water.
You are an ugly duckling.
Go away!

The ugly duckling looks into the water.

He can see an ugly duckling.
He says, That is me in the water.
I am ugly.

The ugly duckling is cold and sad.

He comes to a house.

I can go into this house,
he says.
I can get help here.

But there is a big dog
in the house.

The big dog says,
You are an ugly duckling.
You cannot come in.

The ugly duckling sees some rabbits.

He says, Can I play with you?

The rabbits say, No. You are an ugly duckling. We do not want to play with you.

The ugly duckling is sad.

He says, The little ducklings do not like me.
The marsh ducks, the dog and the rabbits do not like me.

The ugly duckling sees a swan.

I want to be like that swan, he says.

The swan is not ugly.

It is winter. It is cold.
There is ice on the water.
The ugly duckling cannot swim.

He cannot crack the ice.

A man sees the ugly duckling.
The ugly duckling cannot
get up.

The man says, You are cold,
ugly duckling.
You can come home with me.

The man has a big house.

The ugly duckling says,
I like this house.
It is not cold.
I can have a home here.

Some children live in the house.

We can have fun with this ugly duckling, they say.

But the children are not good to the ugly duckling.

This is not fun, says the ugly duckling.

He runs away.

The ugly duckling runs to the marsh.

He has a cold little home by the water.

The ugly duckling looks at the ice.
He is sad.

The winter ice goes.
It is spring.

The ugly duckling looks up.
He sees a swan.

I want to fly like that swan,
he says.

He runs and runs.

Yes – he *can* fly!

Look at me, I can fly!

He says to the swan.

Yes, says the swan.
Look into the water.
You are not a duckling.
You are not ugly.

You have grown into a swan.
You can have a home with me.

The ugly duckling looks into the water.

He can see a swan.

He says, That is me in the water.

I am not an ugly duckling.
I am a swan!